BEGINNER READER

RAINBOW
magic™

The Rainbow Fairies

Orchard Beginner Readers are specially created to develop literacy skills, confidence and a love of reading.

To Wilson, who fills each day with colour.

Special thanks to Kristin Earhart

ORCHARD BOOKS
338 Euston Road, London NW1 3BH
Orchard Books Australia
Level 17/207 Kent Street, Sydney, NSW 2000

First published in the USA in 2010 by Scholastic Inc
This edition published in 2014 by Orchard Books

© 2014 Rainbow Magic Limited.
A HIT Entertainment company. Rainbow Magic is a trademark of Rainbow Magic Limited.
Reg. U.S. Pat. & Tm. Off. And other countries.

HiT entertainment

A CIP catalogue record for this book is available from the British Library.

ISBN 978 1 40833 374 7
1 3 5 7 9 10 8 6 4 2

Printed in China

The paper and board used in this paperback are natural recyclable products made from wood grown in sustainable forests. The manufacturing processes conform to the environmental regulations of the country of origin.

Orchard Books is a division of Hachette Children's Books, an Hachette UK company

www.hachette.co.uk

RAINBOW magic™

The Rainbow Fairies

Daisy Meadows

ORCHARD

It is a special day in Fairyland.
Today is the Feast of All Colours,
so the Fairy King and Queen
are having a picnic to celebrate.

YOU ARE INVITED TO
The Feast
of All
Colours

All the fairies are excited, especially the Rainbow Fairies.

Izzy
the Indigo
Fairy

Amber
the Orange
Fairy

Saffron
the Yellow
Fairy

Fern
the Green
Fairy

They get to choose the foods for the picnic.
There are seven Rainbow Fairies,
one for each colour of the rainbow.

Ruby
the Red
Fairy

Heather
the Violet
Fairy

Sky
the Blue
Fairy

They are sisters, and they share
a very important job: filling the world
with colour!

The Rainbow Fairies are busy
in their toadstool cottage.
It is almost time to fill the picnic baskets.

Just then, the fairy sisters
hear a knock at the door.

"Hello, Rainbow Fairies," a voice croaks.
"Bertram!" the sisters exclaim.
Bertram the frog is a royal messenger
and also their good friend.

"The king asked me to clean your wands," says Bertram.
"Of course," Ruby replies.
"They need to work well for the feast," Izzy agrees.

The fairies hand their wands to Bertram,
who wipes them with a magic cloth.
As the fairies talk about the foods they
will pick, Bertram's stomach growls.

"Excuse me," says the frog.
"I can't wait for the picnic!
The food will be delicious!"

Bertram returns the wands to
the fairies, one by one.

But he isn't thinking about wands.
He is thinking about the feast.

"Thank you, Bertram," the fairies say.
"I am happy to help!" he replies.
"I'll see you at the picnic!"

The fairies carry the empty picnic baskets outside to the meadow.
"What a beautiful day for a picnic!" Fern exclaims.

"But it isn't a picnic without food," insists
Saffron.
Heather says, "Let's get started!"

"I'll go first," says Ruby.
She thinks of her favourite red foods.

"Strawberries, tomatoes and cherries!" Ruby says.
Sparkles stream from her wand into one of the picnic baskets.

Now it's Amber's turn.
She flicks her wand.
"Sweet potatoes, carrots and tangerines!"
she calls out.

"I'm next," says Saffron.
"Corn on the cob with butter! And lemonade!"
Sparkles stream into the basket.
"Now for green," Fern says. "Broccoli, peas and cool cucumber soup, please!"

"Blueberry pie!" Sky declares happily.
"Blackberries!" sings Izzy.
"Grape jam!" exclaims Heather.
Sparkles fly from their wands and spin
through the air.

"Hooray!" cry the fairies. "The picnic is
ready!"
"Let's go home and wash our hands before
the feast," Ruby says.

Just as the fairies leave, someone arrives early for the feast.

It's Bertram, and he's hungry!
He tiptoes up to a picnic basket, lifts the
cover, and looks inside.
"Oh, no!" he cries.

Ruby rushes out of the cottage. "What's the matter, Bertram?"

Bertram points to the baskets and Ruby looks inside.

"Red corn on the cob? Blue strawberries? Violet tangerines?" she mumbles.

"What went wrong?" Bertram asks. "That food does not look delicious."
Ruby's eyes grow wide. "We must have used the wrong wands!" she realises.
"I have to call my sisters!"
Ruby points her wand straight up and blue sparkles shoot into the air.

Soon, the other Rainbow Fairies return to the meadow.

"We got back the wrong wands after Bertram cleaned them," Ruby explains. "And the picnic foods are all the wrong colours!"
"Can we fix them?" Sky asks.

"We need to work together," Ruby says.
"We need Rainbow Magic! And fast!
The king and queen are coming!"
At once, the sisters make a circle.

They hold their wands up high and
speak together:
"Rainbow colours, bold and bright,
The picnic foods are just not right.
Now each wand must find its fairy
To stop the picnic looking scary."

The wands spin around in the air, and each one lands in the hand of its fairy. Just then, sparkles of every colour shimmer and swirl through the meadow.

"What a beautiful beginning to the Feast of All Colours!" announces the king.
"The food looks delicious," the queen says.

"Yes, it does," agrees Bertram, winking at the Rainbow Fairies.
Everyone sits down to enjoy a colourful feast. They have a lot to celebrate!